DUMA™

The Movie Novel

DUMA™

The Movie Novel

by Kathleen Weidner Zoehfeld

Screenplay by Karen Janszen and
Mark St. Germain

Story by Carol Flint and Karen Janszen

Based on the Book
How It Was with Dooms
by Carol Cawthra Hopcraft and
Xan Hopcraft

HarperKidsEntertainment
An Imprint of HarperCollinsPublishers

1

One spring day, on the slope of a mountain in the Erongo Mountain Range, a fluffy brown cheetah cub wrestled with his brothers and sisters. His mama lay nearby in the tall grass. She purred contentedly, keeping watch over her lively brood as the warm sun inched up over the eastern hills. A flock of birds settled in the branches of a fever tree and began singing its morning song.

But the morning's peace did not last long. With a thundering whoosh, the birds suddenly took flight, and the mother cheetah stood up, alert. Before she could move her cubs to safety, two huge lions sprang out of the grass and flung their bodies against hers. She twisted free and began to run, hoping to distract the lions' attention from her helpless cubs.

The little brown cub scurried off in a panic and dove into the thornbushes. As he hunkered down, he spotted lion legs just a few feet away. The lion stalked forward slowly, looking for the slightest movement in the grass. The little cub's heart raced, but he stayed perfectly still. Baffled, the lions finally gave up and moved away. The little cub chirped for his mama. He listened for her answering chirp, but he heard nothing. He scrambled out of the sheltering bushes and began to walk through the endless sea of grass, searching for any sign of his family.

At nightfall he found himself facing a strange barrier. He pressed his nose against the cold metal of a chain-link fence. He ran along the length of it, first to the left and then to the right, but it seemed to stretch on endlessly. He looked up to see if he might climb it, but it was nearly as high as the moon above. Finally, he found an opening just big enough for his head. Where his head could fit, the rest of his body would follow! He wiggled through the tiny opening and fell onto the bare ground on the other side. The little cub had tumbled into a whole new world.

For the first time in his life, he felt smooth asphalt under his paws. A bright yellow line caught his attention, and he lowered his head to lick it. Suddenly, he heard a terrible roar, unlike any lion's roar he'd ever heard. He looked up to see two orbs of light bearing down on him. The little cub froze.

"Dad, back there! We hit him!" cried Xan.

Xan's dad, Peter, had seen him, too. He slammed on the brakes, and they climbed out of their vintage Porsche. "Naw! He's fine. He's here somewhere. . . ."

Peter saw the cub dart away.

"There he is! Get around the other side!" he cried.

"A truck's coming!" shouted Xan.

The cub froze again in the truck's headlights.

"Xan! Quick! Bag the little guy."

Xan grabbed his fishing net. As the cub leaped out of the way of the oncoming truck, he lowered the net over him.

"Yeah, you're fast, but not fast enough," said

Peter, looking at the cub fondly. He reached in and grabbed him. "How the devil did you get out here, fella?"

"He's shaking like a leaf," he told Xan. "Do you see his mama anywhere?"

"I think he's lost," said Xan.

Peter handed the cub to his son. Xan held the little ball of fur up and gazed into his amber eyes. "Hey, you."

Xan and his dad were on their way home from a fishing trip in the Erongo Mountains. They hadn't been too successful, and the bamboo fishing creel they had brought to carry home their catch was empty. Xan pulled it out of the backseat and gently placed the cub inside—it would make the perfect basket for the new baby!

A diner soon came into view on the long,

deserted highway, and they decided to stop. The waitress brought out a Coke for Xan and a coffee with some powdered creamer for his dad. Xan set the basket down on the seat beside him and covered it gently with his jacket.

Peter checked out the waitress's name tag and smiled charmingly. "Thandi, could I trouble you for some real cream?" he asked.

"Wish you could, but we ran out," replied Thandi.

"I can't spoil your good coffee with anything less than the best," flattered Peter.

Thandi smiled. "Lucille! Any milk back there?"

"Not a drop," came the reply.

"Can you point me toward a cow?" Peter joked.

Xan rolled his eyes in embarrassment.

"How about some ice cream," suggested Thandi.

"Thandi, you're a genius!" exclaimed Peter. "Well done!"

"Dad!" whined Xan. "Do you have to talk to everybody?"

"Six billion people in the world, son. I'm doing my best."

Using an empty saltshaker and one of the plastic flowers on the table, Peter created a makeshift baby bottle. He poured in some of the melted ice cream.

"Dad, that'll never work," groaned Xan. His dad handed it to him anyway. Xan shrugged and lowered the bottle into the creel. Slowly, the cub began to lick the flower "nipple."

"He's taking it!" cried Xan. He looked at the little cub's face and saw the distinctive black streaks running from the cub's eyes, down along his nose, and curving around to his mouth. "Look, Dad," he said, "black streaks. You know what that means?"

"A cheetah!" cried Peter.

"Fastest animal alive," said Xan. "Zero to sixty in like two seconds. Faster than your Porsche."

Peter could see a bond forming already between his son and this rare and beautiful cub. "Xan, you can't keep him," he warned, "not forever . . . not anymore than Mom and I can keep you. We can help you grow up, get you ready for the world. But he's a wild animal. One day that's the world he's got to go back to."

Xan ignored his dad and concentrated on feeding the cub.

The waitress leaned over, curious. "What you got in there?"

Xan snapped the creel closed.

"Snake," said Peter. "Want to see?"

The waitress backed up and waved them on their way.

Peter drove all that night. The next day he and Xan arrived at the little town of Patterfield, South Africa. Soon they spotted the familiar turnoff for the long, bumpy, dirt road that would take them home to their farm. Xan rubbed the sleep from his eyes and straightened the creel in his lap. He couldn't wait to show his mom what they had found!

2

"**M**om, hurry! He's got Dad by the throat!"

Kristin dropped her reading glasses and raced down the hall. "*What!?*"

"*Help, Xan! Help!*" cried Peter, making loud sputtering noises.

"*Don't eat him! Nooooo!*" cried Xan.

Kristin burst into the kitchen, only to find her husband lying on the floor, holding the tiny cub in the air above him.

Charlie, their African gray parrot, squawked "Help! Help!" from his perch, adding to the commotion.

"Get him off me!" cried Peter dramatically.

Xan took the cub and snuggled it against his cheek, laughing.

"Whew, that was a close one," joked Peter.

Kristin laughed. "Not nearly close enough!" She knelt down and cuddled the cub. "I'm glad I'm not his mama," she said. "I'd be heartbroken to lose him."

That night, Xan put the cub in a cozy basket in his room, between the caged lizards, the snake, and the insects he had collected on his wanderings around the farm. But the tired cub still chirped pitifully for his mama. Xan lifted him out of the box and put him on his pillow. He stroked the cub gently until he purred, and they both drifted off to sleep.

For the first few months, Xan and his parents kept the cub indoors. Outside, there were just too many dangers for a small, tumbly cheetah. Every day he lapped up cow's milk and raw egg from his bowl. He grew quickly, exploring every nook and cranny of the house—pouncing on the piano keys or watching Charlie the parrot dropping nutshells into his bowl.

Xan's dad named the cub *Duma*, which is Swahili for "cheetah." But Duma was more than just a pet. Before long, he had become like another member of the Van der Bok family. Because the Van der Bok's farm was far from the nearest school, Xan did all his schooling at home with the help of his mom. While Xan studied, Duma played at his feet. He loved to wrestle with Xan's slippers and pounce on his papers, distracting him from his lessons.

One day, when Duma was being especially distracting, Xan's mom came over and tapped his text book. "Back to your poets, Xan," she said.

But Xan thought it was his mom's turn for a challenge. He read to her from his book: "Two roads diverged in a wood, and I, I took the one less traveled by. And that . . . ?" He paused, waiting for her to finish the famous quote.

". . . and that has made all the difference." Kristin beamed triumphantly. She waited for her prize.

Xan nodded. He reached into his pocket and pulled out their favorite African talisman—a small, carved mask with hollow eyes. He tossed it to her, and she caught it in one hand.

"I'll get it back!" he promised.

Kristin kissed the top of her son's head and tucked the talisman into her own pocket.

Charlie the parrot made smoochy noises. Duma purred contentedly.

Those were the happiest times of Xan's young life. When Duma was about four months old, he was finally allowed out on the farm. And from then on, wherever Xan went and whatever he did, Duma was at his side. Duma grew up among the sheep and hens, running and tumbling with Xan through the golden fields of wheat.

3

For months, Xan had been begging his dad to teach him how to drive his motorcycle, and finally the time had come. The bike was big and fast, and it had a sidecar that Xan had always ridden in until now. Duma eyed Xan with curiosity as, instead of climbing in the sidecar, he straddled the big, rumbling machine.

"Gentle, ease it up, ease it up," Peter coaxed.

Grrkkkkk! Xan ground the gears, and Duma cringed. With a slow, jerking motion, the motorcycle began to inch forward. Gradually getting the hang of it, Xan circled around the field, shifting into second and then into third while his dad cheered him on. Before long, Xan was an expert driver, and he could go anywhere on the farm by himself. Duma was learning to sprint faster and faster, too. Every day he enjoyed racing Xan to the top of their favorite hill, where they could see the whole ranch spread out before them.

One day they were on the hilltop playing catch with a soccer ball, when something terrible happened. They could see Peter hard at work plowing the fields below. The tractor came to a stop, and Xan saw his dad climb down to adjust the blades of the plow. But as he was stepping back to his seat, he suddenly crumpled to the ground. Xan and Duma rushed to his aid.

A few days later, Peter came home from the hospital with his hair closely shaved and a big surgical scar on the side of his head. Everything in the Van der Bok household changed. It was many months before Peter felt better. During that time, Duma grew to his adult size. At 6 feet long and 125 pounds, he was almost twice the size of Xan!

Xan's parents didn't talk much about his dad's illness, and Xan's days were sometimes long and lonely. He wiled away many afternoons listening to rap music on his CD player and trying, unsuccessfully, to coax Duma into the swimming pool. Duma absolutely refused to swim. Running was more to his liking. In fact, Xan could hardly believe how fast his best friend had become. He made the motorcycle seem slow! Xan was eager to show his dad how much progress Duma had made.

As soon as he was feeling up to it, Peter suggested that they time Duma and capture his graceful run on video. For the first time in months, Peter took the driver's seat on the motorcycle and raced it across the field. Xan, seated in the sidecar, trained his video camera on the beautiful cat running easily alongside them.

"There it is! Look at that stride!" cried Peter. "We're at sixty! How fast can he go?"

Xan held on tight and kept the camera rolling.

Duma shifted into cheetah overdrive and passed them easily.

Peter pressed the old motorcycle hard to keep up. "Seventy . . . seventy-five. . . eighty. . . incredible!" he cried. "Look at him! Brilliant, Duma! Brilliant!"

With his burst of energy expended, Duma

pulled up, panting heavily. He plopped to the ground and rolled on his back like a big, lazy house cat. It was a thrilling moment, but even though his dad seemed exhilarated, Xan couldn't help seeing the look of deep concern in his eyes.

Later that day, while Xan and Duma were resting in the tree house Xan and his dad had built the year before, Peter came knocking. "Got room up there?" he asked.

Xan lifted the floor hatch and watched his father puff wearily up the ladder with a rolled-up paper in his hand.

Peter looked around at his son's handiwork. While his dad was sick, Xan had put in a new window and a shelf for his books.

"Nice work," said Peter, stroking Duma till he purred.

Xan felt proud, but he knew something else was coming.

"It's time," said Peter. "We have to talk about Duma. He's almost grown up—"

"But Duma's—" Xan interrupted.

"—nearly too old to survive out there," declared Peter. "We have to take him back."

"He doesn't want to go!" cried Xan. "He doesn't want to be wild."

"You can't decide that for him," said Peter. "His wildness is something he knows without knowing. It's in his blood—in his bones, like a memory."

Xan did not want to understand.

"Like how I know I belong here, on my father's farm," Peter continued.

"There are hardly any cheetahs left," Xan argued. "There's no place for him."

Peter smiled. "But there is."

He unrolled the paper, and Xan saw it was a map of southern Africa. His father pointed to their home in Patterfield. "We're here," he said, "and we found him . . . here." He traced a path across the Makgadikgadi Salt Flats, through the Okavango Delta, and on to the spot in the Erongo Mountains where they had gone fishing. "And just north of there are mountains and a beautiful valley with a little river. Lots of springbok and gazelle! Big cat heaven!"

"Lions!" cried Xan. "He'll get eaten by lions! Or he'll starve. He can't catch a mouse."

"He'll learn," said Peter. "Chase, trip, and bite. How hard can it be?"

Xan had seen cheetahs hunting on nature programs on TV, and it didn't look all that easy to him!

"We'll camp out," said Peter. "It'll be great."

Xan looked at his father skeptically. "Why now?"

Deep down, Peter knew he might not have many summers left to go camping with his son.

"Why not?" he said, trying to sound lighthearted.

Xan scowled and stared into Duma's endless eyes.

"Duma has to live the life he was born into," said his father, "or he'll never be fully alive. It's part of growing up. He has to find out who he is and where he belongs."

▲ ▼ ▲ ▼ ▲ ▼ ▲ ▼ ▲ ▼ ▲ ▼ ▲ ▼

4

Over the next few weeks, Peter grew weaker and weaker. On good days, he wrapped up in his warmest bathrobe and sat on the porch with Duma, looking into the wild cat's knowing eyes. On bad days, he didn't even get out of bed.

With their camping plans on hold, Xan tried to concentrate on his schoolwork. He recited from his poetry text, "From too much love of living, / From hope and fear set free, / We thank with brief thanksgiving / Whatever gods may be . . ."

Kristin listened. He was reading too fast and stumbling over the words. "Pause after each line," she advised him. "Read it like you're singing a song. The sound of the words is the melody."

Xan took a breath and continued more slowly. "That no life lives for ever; / That dead men rise up never; / That even the weariest river / Winds somewhere safe to sea."

He looked up from his book, hoping for praise. But his mom was staring at the floor. He thought he saw tears welling up in her eyes.

"Mom?"

"I'm sorry," she replied.

Xan wished she'd tell him what she was sorry about. He wished she would talk about what was happening to Dad, and to their family, but she checked herself and teased him instead. "Tell me something. Without looking. What shoes are you wearing?"

Xan grinned. "Um . . ." He pretended to think. "No shoes."

They looked down at Xan's feet. He was right: only socks. Kristin took the talisman from her pocket and tossed it to him. He caught it, laughing.

"I'll get it back," she promised.

Early one morning, Xan was awakened by strange voices and commotion in the house. Red lights flashed across the ceiling of his room. He ran out into the hall to find paramedics taking his father away on a stretcher. His mom grabbed him and held him close.

A few days later, they held his dad's funeral in town, and afterward family and friends gathered around his grave in the Van der Bok family cemetery.

Xan felt lost and alone. Dinners went by in pained silence, with Peter's empty chair like a grim, ghostly presence and Duma looking on from his corner with his somber eyes.

During the day, Xan sat at the pool's edge, making little circles on the water's surface. Duma lay beside him, swishing his tail. Every now and then it would accidentally dip into the water, and he'd shake the drops off, annoyed. Xan knew the cat needed to run, but neither of them seemed to have the energy to get up and go.

Kristin came and sat beside them. She looked at her son for a long time, trying to find the words. "Honey," she said, "we're making some changes."

"Like what?" asked Xan.

Kristin took a long breath. "I have to lease the farm."

Xan tried to figure out what she meant. "But we'll still live in the house, right?"

"No." His mom shook her head, sadly. "We're going to the city, to live with Aunt Gwen for a while. I can get a job—"

"What about Duma?" Xan cried.

Kristin tried to sound upbeat. "Duma will get a new home, too. A great big preserve where he'll have plenty of room—"

"That's not what Dad wanted!"

Kristin sighed. "I have to take care of us, and the only way I can do that is to—"

Xan flung himself into the water, making a giant splash. He sat on the bottom of the pool, stubbornly struggling to hold his breath. When he thought his lungs were about to burst, he rose up and took a gulp of air.

"Xan!" cried his mom.

He dove back under.

She jumped in after him, clothes and all.

He shot up to the surface, pulling away from her and shouting, "Nooooo!"

"Xan, I can't do this alone," she pleaded. "Your father and I talked about this. About what to do . . . after. It's the only thing that makes sense."

Xan clung to the side of the pool and buried his head in his arms. A preserve? He couldn't believe what he was hearing. How could his dad have left him—and left Duma, too—alone, with no way back to his real home?

For my mom Susan Elizabeth
Quigley Bateman.

5

Two weeks later, they had loaded their things in the old family Range Rover. Kristin was driving them to her sister's apartment in Johannesburg. Sporting his new red leather collar, Duma sat in the backseat next to Charlie's covered birdcage, the lizards' cage, and the snake's vivarium.

Xan stared glumly out the window, as the glittering urban skyline of Johannesburg appeared on the horizon.

"I know this is scary," said his mom. "I know it won't be easy. But I wouldn't be moving us if I didn't think we could both adapt and make a new life here."

Xan just stared in silence.

"We can do this if we stick together," Kristin pleaded.

He pulled his CD headphones over his ears, turned up the volume, and tuned her out.

The next few days were even worse than Xan had imagined. Aunt Gwen welcomed them into her apartment, but she had no idea what to make of Duma. He looked forlornly out the window at parking lots and city walls. Aunt Gwen was uneasy.

"The man from the preserve will be here in a day or two," Kristin reassured her.

Xan put on his blazer and tie for his first day at

a real school—Sunninghill Junior High. He looked at himself in the mirror—his shirt was already rumpled and his tie was a crooked mess.

When he and his mom arrived at school, all he could see were crowds of kids, laughing and shouting to one another. He opened the Rover's door to get out, a big knot forming in his stomach.

"Xan, wait," said his mom.

He stopped and glanced back at her, impatiently. "What?" he huffed.

"All you have to do today is look around—get the lay of the land," she advised. "You're strong and you're smart and you have a big heart. Those kids don't know anything you don't know."

He smiled, grateful for her encouragement. Then he marched like a soldier toward his doom, determined to do the best he could.

Before he knew it, it was afternoon and he was facing gym class in his white shirt and tie. All the other kids had donned their red gym shorts and official Sunninghill T-shirts. Could he look any more like The New Kid? He pretended not to notice that a group of pretty girls were giggling at him.

On the other side of the playground, Hock Bender, the school bully, was looking him over. "Gentlemen," he said to his buddies, "our day is made."

At the same time Hock and his pals were making their spiteful plans, back at the apartment Kristin made a decision. She pulled on a sweater. "I'm going to pick up Xan," she called to her sister as she headed out the door.

Duma sprang to attention.

Alone in the apartment with the cat for the first time, Aunt Gwen was nervous. Duma sniffed around, exploring all the nooks and crannies. From between two couch cushions he rooted out an old pretzel. He decided the TV remote might make a good snack, too. *Chomp!* The TV zapped on. *Chomp, Chomp!* A cartoon blasted at top volume. "I t'ought I taw a puddy tat!" boomed Tweety bird.

Duma jumped away in a panic, knocking over a small table and lamp. Aunt Gwen flew out of the apartment, screaming. Duma cautiously considered the open door. As he peered outside, he caught sight of Kristin pulling out in the familiar Range Rover. He raced after it.

At the house next door, a young mother was ready to take her two-year-old daughter for a walk in her stroller. The little girl pointed at Duma. "Kitty, kitty!" she squealed happily.

"Here he is," said the mother, without looking up. She handed her daughter a stuffed kitten.

Duma sped past joggers and commuters. All around him brakes squealed and cars swerved, barely avoiding collisions. Duma paid no attention. He was intent on catching up with Kristin and the Range Rover.

Meanwhile, Xan had moved on to his social studies class. His teacher looked on sternly as a student read his mind-bogglingly dull report on the Egyptian pyramids. Xan was wondering how it was possible to make such a cool subject so boring, when he caught a glimpse of Duma moving past the window.

Xan grabbed his things and headed for the door.

"Excuse me, young man," said the teacher. "Where are you going?"

"Out there," said Xan, gesturing toward the window.

"Out there?" echoed the teacher sarcastically.

The students snickered.

"Aaahhhhhhhh!!!!!!" They heard kids screaming down the hall. The students hushed and listened.

"Nobody leaves my room without my permission," snapped the teacher, oblivious of the hubbub outside.

As the screams drew nearer, the students started fidgeting, not knowing whether to run or to stay put.

Xan shot out the door. All around him students were running in a panic. The fire alarm began to blare.

"Fire drill!" yelled another teacher. "Exit row by row! Stay orderly, please!"

But Xan's class piled out the door in a big chaotic heap. Xan pressed himself up against a wall to get his bearings. Outside the hall window, he saw two police cars pulling up. The police got out, carrying shotguns.

Xan saw the flash of a spotted tail swishing down the hall and turning through a doorway. He ran to catch up, struggling against his fellow students who were all running the other way. It looked as though Duma had gone into the boys' bathroom. Xan opened the door and called. "Duma? You in here?"

He began to open stall doors, peering into each one.

Suddenly, he heard a voice mocking him.

"Who's Duma? Your boyfriend?"

Xan looked over to see Hock and his buddies smoking cigarettes by the sinks. Xan froze.

Hock pointed to the CD player hanging around Xan's neck. "That. Very nice."

"My father gave it to me," said Xan lamely.

"And you're going to give it to me," sneered Hock, "or pay me to let you keep it." He waved a big wad of cash under Xan's nose. Hock's two henchmen moved in close to back him up. There was no escape. *Wham!* Hock punched Xan in the nose. Xan tried to hold on to his CD player and swing back. But Hock and his two minions knocked him over and pinned him down. With his cheek squashed to the floor, Xan spied four spotted feet under a stall door. The familiar feet were moving toward him.

Grrrrrrrrrrrrr . . .

Hock and his buddies froze. They let go of Xan and slowly turned to face the strange noise.

Duma growled louder and crouched as if to pounce. He hissed, opening his mouth wide and flashing his sharp teeth.

The terrified boys dashed out of the bathroom, leaving their big wad of cash behind.

Xan picked it up, impressed. "Well done, Duma!"

By the time he and Duma emerged from the bathroom, the hallway was eerily quiet. They tiptoed for the exit. One of the police officers caught sight of Duma's hindquarters disappearing around a corner. He raised his gun and took a shot.

Duma began to run. Xan struggled to keep him in view. He could see Duma streaking ahead of him, across the basketball court, away from the school, down a street crowded with traffic.

Kristin was in the school parking lot, trying to figure out what all the panic was about. She spotted Xan headed for the busy street.

"Xan! Wait!" she cried, running after him.

Xan followed Duma through a crowded outdoor market and then into a small park where the cheetah disappeared. "Duma?" he whispered.

Hearing his name, Duma poked his furry head out the window of a small tree house.

"Come on, Duma. We've got to get out of here."

A Recreation Department truck was parked on the road nearby. Xan saw two big wire trash barrels in the back of the truck and decided to make his move. He coaxed Duma onto the truck and into one of the barrels. Peering out from behind trash and gardening supplies, Xan and Duma watched the Recreation Department employees loading up their truck for the day. They pulled into the maintenance yard and parked.

Xan waited till everyone had gone home. Then he and Duma crept out of hiding and made their way past the long line of parked trucks and through the chain-link fence surrounding the yard. They sat on a hill overlooking the busy highway and the big noisy city, trying to decide what to do.

"Duma, we have to go far away. Go home, like Dad said." Xan made Duma sit quietly behind a building as he flagged down a cab. As soon as the driver stopped, Xan opened the door and motioned for Duma to hop in.

"Patterfield, please," said Xan.

The driver stared in his mirror at the big cat looming in the backseat. "That's a very long ride." He gulped.

"I know," said Xan. He pointed at Duma, who was staring right back at the driver. "And he's really in a hurry."

▲ ▼ ▲ ▼ ▲ ▼ ▲ ▼ ▲ ▼ ▲ ▼ ▲ ▼

6

The Van der Bok house was dark and quiet when Xan and Duma arrived. The electricity had been turned off. He and his mom had draped all the furniture in sheets, and now they looked like ghosts in the moonlight. Still, it felt good to be home.

Xan opened his father's closet and took out his well-worn backpack. He loaded it with the essential gear—a compass, lighter, knife, and the map his dad had shown him in the tree house. As he was cinching the pack closed, he heard the sound of a car approaching and saw lights flashing through the window. Xan pulled Duma out the back door, and they crouched behind the chicken coop.

"Xan? You out there?"

Xan heard his mother's voice calling. He rose to greet her. But as he came around the corner of the coop, he spotted a police officer with a shotgun walking beside her.

Kristin didn't notice Xan in the darkness, and she continued to call. "Xan? It's okay. Please believe me."

But Xan could see a police car pulling around the house. He grabbed Duma and ducked deeper into the darkness.

"Xan!" shouted Kristin, unable to believe her

son was not there.

The police officer gently encouraged her to get back in the car. It seemed clear that her son was elsewhere. They drove off, alerting all patrol cars to keep on the lookout for a young boy, possibly accompanied by a cheetah.

At dawn, Xan strapped his pack on his dad's motorcycle. Duma climbed into the sidecar, and they were off—rap music blasting from the CD player. Xan grinned, triumphant in his freedom.

They'd only gotten a few miles down the road, though, when Xan saw the red lights of a police car up ahead. He zipped into a gas station and parked behind a big truck. Duma waited patiently in the sidecar while Xan bought them some food for the road—popcorn, chewing gum, bottles of water, and, for Duma, some rare roast beef.

On and on they sped, down the long, desolate road. They came to a turnoff, and Xan checked his compass. It was a narrow dirt road heading toward the harsh scrubland. Northwest. Xan sighed. It was an awful road, but that was their direction.

By evening they had crossed a dry, sandy riverbed. They followed the dusty track up the steep bank. But as they looked out over the top of the rise, the road seemed to vanish into a wide landscape of scrub brush and gnarly trees.

Suddenly, Xan spotted dark shapes emerging from the bushes. A bunch of yellow eyes gleamed in the light of his motorcycle headlight. In his terror Xan stepped on the gas and zoomed past. His tires skidded in a rut, and before he knew it the bike went tumbling off the road, sending him and Duma flying head over heels into the bushes.

The motorcycle engine sputtered to a stop, and the whole world seemed to go dark and silent. Taking a moment to come to his senses, Xan gazed at the stars glittering overhead and listened to the whining of mosquitoes.

"I say we stop for the night," he said to the air. Duma watched as Xan gathered their few belongings near the motorcycle.

The cheetah draped himself on a sturdy branch and stared wide-eyed into the dark sky. As the night wore on, Xan tossed and turned in the boughs beside him. Far off, they could hear the hyenas cackling. Then, a hyena scream. Then, a lion's roar.

"Sorry," whispered Xan. "I didn't think this far." He put his arms around Duma, and they tried to sleep.

As soon as the sun came up, they were off again. At the top of a long hill Xan pulled the motorcycle to a stop. Gone were the bushes and scraggly trees. Spread out before them was an empty endless stretch of red sand dunes. Xan consulted his map. "We started here . . ." he muttered, pointing to Patterfield. He traced his finger a little way across the map. "Was that the river we rode over?" he asked, dismayed. "Then we're only . . ."

Duma gnawed on an old chew toy and stretched his front paws over the map.

"Hey, get off the Erongo Mountains!" cried Xan.

Duma inched over a little.

Xan moved his finger over the route his father had drawn—across desert, jungle, and grasslands—and considered the immensity of the journey ahead. "A lot of map to go." He sighed. He stared into Duma's amber eyes. "Should we keep going?"

Duma stood and walked toward the dunes. He stopped and glanced back over his shoulder at Xan.

"That's what I think, too," said Xan.

They took off, the motorcycle humming, Duma running beside it. They crossed the red desert, zigzagging through the dunes, rap music blaring from the CD player.

When they came to the edge of the great salt pans of the Makgadikgadi, Xan stopped to consider this uninviting new landscape. The vast, treeless plain glistened bone white in the hot African sun. Panting, Duma climbed into the sidecar. Xan slumped in the driver's seat—a sun-baked, rumpled mess. And the two pals pressed on. Then, in the middle of that barren no-man's-land, the motorcycle's engine sputtered to a halt. Xan tapped the gas gauge. *Empty.*

"It was gonna happen sooner or later." Xan sighed. He pulled out a water bottle and some cold cuts. "I was hoping for later."

Duma snapped up a slice of roast beef and lapped up a few drops of water.

"Enjoy it," said Xan. "You're catching your next meal yourself."

Xan unwrapped a Tootsie Roll and stared at the dead motorcycle. When he'd finished his "meal," he folded the map up into a kind of Napoleonic hat. He grabbed the motorcycle's handlebars and began to push. Duma stayed put in his sidecar. Xan rolled his eyes at him. "Do you even know what 'wild' means?"

The fierce sun beat down on them, and the wind howled. Eventually, Xan made Duma get out of the sidecar. Step after agonizing step, their feet crunched on the salt. Duma was beginning to limp. Xan was parched. They stopped and stared, overwhelmed by the enormity of their predicament. Scanning the horizon, Duma perked up his head. When Xan followed his gaze, he saw something protruding from the flat salt landscape.

As they trudged closer, he saw that it was the tail of an airplane and part of the fuselage, jutting from the salt pan like the skeleton of some extinct monster. When they finally got to the plane, Xan had enough energy to poke around the wreckage for only a few minutes. Then he and Duma flopped down in its shade, wetting their lips with a few precious drops of water. "That's it until tomorrow," said Xan.

As they watched the sun go down, Xan unwrapped the last Tootsie Roll and tried to share it with Duma. Duma tested a bite and then spat it out on the salt. Xan considered picking it up and eating it himself. Nah, too yucky.

Later that evening, as Xan was trying to sleep on one of the airplane's mangled seats, Duma turned to consider the discarded piece of Tootsie Roll once more.

Right before his eyes a small bony hand reached out and grabbed the candy. Duma's eyes followed the little hand to the creature's mouth. Above that were two big staring eyes. The animal popped the Tootsie Roll in his mouth and blinked. Duma crouched to spring.

Spotting Duma's motion, the creature leaped up to a safe perch high on the airplane's tail. He chewed on his sweet treat, satisfied. Duma eyed him and sulked. He put his chin down on the hard salt pan, and before long he was fast asleep.

▲ ▼ ▲ ▼ ▲ ▼ ▲ ▼ ▲ ▼ ▲ ▼ ▲ ▼ ▲ ▼

7

"**E**eeek! Eeeek!" The odd little animal on the airplane's tail shrieked, and Duma's eyes popped open. The sun was already red on eastern horizon, and Duma noticed a dark figure moving toward them out of the glow.

Duma growled softly and moved close to Xan, who was still asleep. The figure drew closer, and Duma growled again—louder this time.

Xan snapped to attention. He heard the crunching of footsteps on the salt. Then more noises—it sounded as if someone was trying to start his motorcycle!

"Hey! What are you doing?!" he shouted. He ran to the 'cycle and came face-to-face with a looming, bearded giant of a man.

"Going south. Got a problem?" the man replied in a smooth, deep voice.

Xan gathered himself up and tried to act as big and grown-up as he could. "Yeah," he declared. "We're going west."

"You and who else?" asked the man.

"My buddy."

At that moment Duma appeared from around the fuselage. He moved close to Xan's side and growled at the stranger.

"Got water?" Xan asked, coolly, trying not to sound desperate.

"Maybe," replied the man. "What you got?"

"The motorcycle. I could give you a ride."

The two eyed each other uneasily. The man was as desperate to get off the pan as Xan was. He tossed him his canteen.

Xan savored a few sips of water and then gave some to Duma.

"Hey!" cried the man. "I only got that little." He tried again to start the motorcycle, but with no luck. "This thing work?"

"It works if you have gas," said Xan.

The man shook his head and laughed. "I am Opuno Kgadi Ripkuna," he introduced himself. "People call me Rip. And you. What are you? An angel or a devil? And how did you end up here?"

Sweating and miserable, Xan and Rip slumped in the shade of the wreck. Xan explained briefly how he and Duma had gotten this far. He didn't quite trust this stranger, but he and Duma weren't doing too well on their own and Rip might be helpful.

Xan shuffled over to see if he could find anything left to eat in his backpack. He opened it up, and the bony-fingered little creature with a peanut stuffed in his mouth popped out like a jack-in-the-box.

"A bush baby!" cried Xan. "How'd it get here?"

"Same as me," said Rip. "Too many wrong turns."

Duma swished his tail impatiently and glared at Rip.

"Your friend doesn't like me," Rip said.

The bush baby scurried over and grabbed Duma's tail. Annoyed, Duma gave it a flick, and the bush baby tumbled away.

Rip laughed. "He don't like nobody but you."

The bush baby jumped on Duma's back. The cheetah shook himself and the bush baby went flying, crashing into the canteen and spilling half the water in the process.

"Oh, no!" exclaimed Xan.

Rip nodded in agreement. "*Mashaka*. Mischievous. A troublemaker."

"*Mashaka*," repeated Xan.

The bush baby looked up at Xan with his big, bright eyes.

"You name him, he becomes your responsibility," said Rip. He paused for a moment. "The cheetah," he asked, "he can use his nose or ears . . . to smell water or hear people talk?"

"Hardly," said Xan.

"There is a big river. Maybe a five-day walk. But to get there, we must have food. . . ." Rip pointed at Duma and then at Mashaka. "Which one?"

"Which one what?"

"Which one we eat first?"

Xan stared at Rip in disbelief.

"For us to live, we have to eat them, drink their blood!"

Duma inched closer to Xan.

"After that, we decide which of us eats the other," Rip explained. "You think about it. We got a day or so before we decide."

Xan stroked Duma nervously. Now, it seemed, he had even more to worry about!

Rip shook the last few drops of water out of his canteen. "No water. No food. No plan. No good."

But as Xan watched the fierce desert wind

whipping old bits of cloth and loose debris from the airplane, he came up with an idea.

Working long into the night, he and Rip cobbled together an old parachute and some junk from the airplane into a sail for the motorcycle. The runaway boy and the outcast man were a good team. They worked fast, and the next morning, with skies blue and wind blowing, they were ready to try Xan's invention.

"Wait, hold it! Duma!" shouted Xan.

"Come on, man! I can't hold it!" Rip shouted back.

The motorcycle took off by itself!

They ran to catch up. Rip grabbed the rickety contraption and held onto it with all his might. "Get on!" he cried.

Xan jumped aboard and Rip clambered in

behind him. Faster and faster they flew, with Duma racing to catch up. Rip's hand slipped from the handlebars, and the 'cycle spun out. Duma took the opportunity to hop on. Rip maneuvered the 'cycle back under control. He was getting the hang of it. Before long they were sailing smoothly over the salt like an old Spanish galleon. They whooped and shouted in glee!

"Which way are we going?" asked Xan.

"There is only one way—the way the wind blows! West!"

8

The strong salt-flat wind blew their makeshift Makgadikgadi Express across the deserted expanse and straight to the Kalahari desert. *Whump!* The motorcycle came to an abrupt stop against a scrubby bush. But the bush was a welcome sight—the first plant they had seen in days!

"Now we find a river!" exclaimed Rip. "Straight up!"

Xan stared out at the brittle-dry brush of the

Kalahari. "There's no water here." He sighed.

Rip was already heading toward a dry riverbed. "You can't see it! You got to smell it!"

Xan and Duma trailed after him. They watched as he dug deep into the sand with his hands.

Rip dug down so far, his arms disappeared up to his shoulders. "*Oh, yes, you see!*" he shouted. He lifted his arms out and showed Xan his wet hands. "Dig! Dig!" he cried.

Xan couldn't believe his eyes. He dropped to his knees and scooped the sand away. The bush baby peered out of Xan's pack and chattered happily. Xan tried to cup some water in his hands, but all he came up with was an undrinkable handful of mud.

Rip pulled a rag from his pack and began to soak up water with it. He raised the rag in his hand

and squeezed, letting the water trickle down his thumb into his open mouth. He fished out another rag for Xan.

When they and the animals had drunk their fill, they sat back and sighed. They had made it to the Kalahari and found water. Now they had to think about food.

Duma spotted it first. He flattened himself to the ground, staring at the ostrich in the distance.

Xan crouched at his side like a coach and whispered, "*Hunt,* Duma! Chase, trip, bite! Go! Go get it!"

Duma turned and gazed at Xan with a blank expression.

"Go!" Xan crouched in the grass and slowly, silently, began padding toward the ostrich. Duma looked excited. He was starting to get it! "Easy . . .

easy . . ." Xan stopped, letting Duma creep forward on his own.

The wary ostrich saw Duma at once and ran off across the sand like a bottom-heavy ballerina. Duma sprinted after the bird, but something else caught his attention. He stopped short and lowered his head to sniff. Xan and Rip ran over to see what Duma had found. Duma had discovered a nest of ostrich eggs!

Rip laughed, unimpressed. "Yeah, he's a hunter. He caught an egg."

That afternoon, Rip cooked a couple of the eggs over a scrub brush campfire. Mashaka chattered, desperate for a bite, but was too scared of the fire to come close enough to grab it. Xan gathered more sticks for the fire.

Rip gestured toward Duma. "He won't stay

alive long out here. For what he's worth you could build a house. Could build a lot of houses. Maybe buy a nice car. . . ."

Xan scowled. "You don't sell a friend." He took his map out of his pack, and Mashaka hopped onto his shoulder.

"The rich, they buy animals like him. Pay big money and make business. Zoo, fun park . . . and make more money."

Trying his best to ignore him, Xan opened the map.

"Where're you going?" asked Rip. "You know?"

"I'm taking Duma home," Xan replied.

"Home?" Rip scoffed. "No such thing! Move here, go there. Nowhere is home. Everywhere is home."

Xan showed Rip the map, pointing to the circle

his dad had drawn. "His home is here, in the mountains."

Xan saw a mysterious expression cross Rip's face.

"Yeah . . . there," he mused. "You sure? That place, it is a very long ways."

"That's where my dad and I found him," said Xan.

Rip raised his eyebrows. "You plan to cross the Okavango?"

"Yeah, so?"

"A place of many teeth. A place to die."

"I'm not afraid," said Xan.

"Be smart!" declared Rip. "Be afraid!"

As the day faded into darkness, they could hear the distant roar of lions.

Duma trembled with fear.

"End up in lion's belly," said Rip, nodding in his direction.

Rip threw more sticks on the fire. "Fire, only thing that will keep you safe out here. Only thing that scares lions." He tapped his finger inside the circle on Xan's map. "I know that place. I can take you a little ways that way. Then, I go back south."

Xan wondered about this strange, scary man. But he had no doubt about it—he would need Rip's help to survive.

▲ ▼ ▲ ▼ ▲ ▼ ▲ ▼ ▲ ▼ ▲ ▼ ▲ ▼ ▲ ▼

9

At about the same time Xan's motorcycle ran out of gas, his mom had returned home to the farm. She knew if she had any hope of finding Xan it would be out there in the wide countryside around Patterfield, not in the city.

It wasn't long before she noticed that the old motorcycle and sidecar were missing. In the barn where they used to stand, she found a note.

Mom,

I'm taking Duma back. I know you will understand—because you are smart and strong and have a big heart.

Love,

Xan

For the first time since Xan had disappeared, Kristin felt a ray of hope, but at the same time she was deeply worried. She knew where her son was now, but how on earth could he survive such a long, dangerous trip on his own? She hurried into the Range Rover and headed off after him.

Meanwhile, as Xan and Rip trudged farther

across the Kalahari, the landscape around them was becoming as dry and barren as the moon.

Duma trotted on ahead. His brush with the ostrich had put him in touch with his hunting instincts for the first time. Now he stood tall and alert in the wide landscape, listening to the call of the jackals, the twittering of the birds, and the hum of the insects. He held his head high and sniffed the air. An interesting scent caught his attention, and he scanned the horizon eagerly.

There they were! A group of giraffes, their heads bobbing over a grove of acacia trees! Duma crouched and quivered.

"Duma!" Xan called.

Duma turned toward the sound of his name. Without a moment's hesitation, he called off the hunt and loped back to Xan's side.

Xan had stopped to check his compass. Rip plopped down to rest in the shade of a rock. Xan frowned. He couldn't tell for sure, but he suspected that they were heading more north than west. Altogether the *wrong* direction for getting Duma home!

Xan kept his worries to himself as they continued. Topping the crest of a high ridge, they were surprised by the sight of a ghost town nestled in a rocky ravine. They made their way to the ruins of an ancient church. On the hill opposite the doorway, they could see the gaping entrance to an old abandoned mine.

Rip shook his head. "This place is full of angry spirits."

To one side of the church was a sandy field littered with bleached bones. The relentless Kalahari wind had uncovered the graves of the people buried there long ago.

"Who are they?" asked Xan.

"People who never dreamed of dying here," replied Rip. "Life, it can have its own plans for you."

Duma crouched and sniffed the ground, nosing into the empty eye sockets of human skulls. As Xan and Rip walked toward him, Rip's foot caught on something in the ground. He bent over and brushed the sand away. It was a large iron spearhead, its tip still embedded in a piece of charred wood.

Rip held the spearhead up with great reverence. "There's a story in this. Not sure I want to know it." He put it in Xan's hand so he could feel the heft of it. "In the right hands, it will kill anything."

Whop-whop-whop-whop-whop-whop! Suddenly, the sound of a helicopter approaching caught their attention, and they searched the sky. There it was, flying over the crest of the mountains! It was moving toward them! As the whirl of the rotor grew louder, Xan ducked down in a ditch, holding Duma close. Rip soon hit the dirt beside them.

The helicopter hovered low over the church for a few seconds and then began to circle the ruined town. Xan craned his neck to see inside the cockpit. A pilot and one passenger. The passenger was leaning out the door anxiously scanning the terrain. No doubt about it—it was his mom! The helicopter hovered close overhead. Xan felt terribly sorry for her, and lonely and frightened for himself. He began to scramble out of the ditch—to call to her! But a big, strong hand grabbed him by the shoulder and yanked him down. Xan shook himself free of Rip's grasp and struggled back up the slope.

It was too late. The helicopter was gone. And his mom was gone with it.

As night fell, Rip built a campfire. He sat up close to it, his eyes gleaming in the firelight, his hands carefully honing the edge of the rusted iron spearhead to a bright sharp sheen.

Xan scowled as he watched Rip. He wondered what secrets Rip was keeping and why he had been so anxious to hide from the helicopter. Xan was too cautious to ask, but his mistrust of this strange man was growing.

Rip attached a strong, straight stick onto the spearhead and held it up for inspection. "An honorable weapon," he declared, "if there is such a thing. For a real warrior. For when you must face your enemy and show your courage, eye to eye."

"Were you ever in the army?" asked Xan.

"Yeah, I'm a major general," replied Rip sarcastically.

He stood up and demonstrated some spearman's moves. "This is to parry your enemy's thrusts away from your vitals. Then when you see the opening—the *thrust*!" He lunged forward, stopping the menacing spear tip just inches from Xan's face.

Xan blinked, motionless.

Duma flattened his ears to his head and backed away.

Rip relaxed his pose. "There are no more warriors. Only cowards with guns."

He jabbed the spear point into the earth and

sat down beside it. He looked over at Xan, concerned. Stubbornly silent, Xan was petting Duma.

"Know how he got those black lines on his face?" asked Rip.

Xan put his fingers on the distinctive marks running down from Duma's eyes. "They cut down glare. Cheetahs hunt in the daytime," he replied, remembering what he'd read in his schoolbooks.

Rip shook his head. "A mother cheetah had a cub she loved dearly. One day he got lost. She searched and searched, and called and called, and cried so long and hard that her tears left black streaks down her face."

Xan couldn't help feeling a little curious. "Did she get her cub back?" he asked.

"A wise man returned him. But her face was stained forever from crying."

Xan and his dad make a new friend.

Duma plays piano.

Duma is part of the family.

Xan and Peter talk about Duma's future.

Xan doesn't exactly fit in at his new school in Johannesburg.

A very scared Duma is completely out of place in the city.

A cross-country journey begins. . . .

Will they make it safely through the desert?

Which way is west?

In the desert, Xan meets Rip.

Best friends.

Xan tries to fend for himself in the forest.

Xan and Duma cross the river on a homemade raft.

Time to say good-bye.

Duma is home at last.

Xan looked at Duma's face. He began to see in it a look of sorrow, passed down through thousands of cheetah generations. He couldn't help thinking of his own mother—out there, somewhere, still frantically searching for him.

Rip seemed satisfied with Xan's reaction. He threw more wood on the fire and lay back with the long spear across his chest.

Xan curled up next to Duma, pretending to sleep, wondering what the new day would bring.

▲ ▼ ▲ ▼ ▲ ▼ ▲ ▼ ▲ ▼ ▲ ▼ ▲ ▼ ▲ ▼

10

The next morning Xan was eager to continue their journey, but Rip insisted they explore the old mine first.

"A lot of diamonds came out of here," he said, "but you know they didn't get them all."

"I want to keep going," Xan complained.

"Just a quick look."

Xan watched Rip work his way down the mine shaft until he was swallowed up by the darkness of the earth. While Rip explored, Xan checked and rechecked his compass and map. Yes, he was sure of it now. They were definitely going in the wrong direction!

From the depths of the mine, Rip's voice sounded small and muffled. "This is a really old one. Lots of smelly old ghosts down here!"

On the spot, Xan made a decision. "Come on," he whispered to Duma. "We're getting out of here."

But as they were tiptoeing away, they felt the earth rumble. A cloud of dust shot out of the mine's entrance. Xan ran back and yelled down the shaft. *"Rip?! You all right?!"*

All he could hear was more rumbling and crashing.

"Rip!" he cried. He started down the collapsing shaft. Sand and debris rained on his head from above. He saw a hand waving desperately out of a

pile of sand and rocks. Rip's! Xan grabbed Rip's shovel and began to dig. Finally, he could see the top of his head. He scooped the dirt away with his hands until he could see his face.

. Rip gasped for air. "Oh, man! Did I ever love to see another!"

"Are you hurt?" asked Xan.

"It happened so fast!" cried Rip. "I'm just happy to breathe. Oh, man!"

Xan dug Rip's arms free.

"Luckily no big stones," said Rip, wiggling his fingers. "Only little stuff."

Xan sat back on his haunches and watched Rip dig himself out. He figured it would take him more than an hour to get completely free by himself. Plenty of time to get away.

"Rip," he asked. "Where're you taking us?"

"Where you want to go."

"No, you're not. We've been going north, not west."

Rip nodded. "The way to the mountains."

"The way to town," declared Xan. "To the police. And money."

"What are you talking about?" cried Rip.

"Collecting a reward for me, and selling Duma."

"How'd you get such ideas?" cried Rip. "We go north to go west. Straight west is the Okavango. We'd all die there!'"

"You just want to scare me," Xan sneered. "You want me to stay with you so you can turn us in. We're going *our* way. You go yours."

Xan tossed Rip the shovel and stormed out of the mine.

"Wait!" Rip called. "You haven't got a chance!"

Xan spotted Rip's spear leaning against his pack and grabbed it. He figured Rip must've been planning to use it to keep him in line. "Let's go, Duma. Hurry!" he cried. "I don't want him following us."

"You're going to be dead meat, boy!" Xan could hear Rip's voice fading as he and Duma went forth into the vast landscape. Seeing them heading away, Mashaka swung down from a bush and followed.

11

Xan marched on like a soldier, water bottle strapped to his backpack and spear in hand. "We're better off without him," he muttered to Duma. "We're doing fine on our own." He punched a hole in a raw egg with a sharp stick and sucked out the yolk. Duma nosed the empty shell.

"Nope," teased Xan. "None for you. You've got to get your own food."

They stopped, and as Xan squinted into the distance, he could see the brown desert giving way to a sea of green grass. By noon they were completely submerged in the tall, dense vegetation. Xan could feel the ground getting squishy under his feet. All around them they heard birds squawking and singing. Brightly colored dragonflies zigzagged overhead.

Before long they came out on the bank of a deep, clear river. Xan sat and pondered how they might get across. Finally, he got up and began gathering branches. He tore his school shirt into strips and used them to tie the branches together.

Duma lay at the water's edge, eyeing a large gray heron that was fishing near the opposite bank. In a rushing, frothy explosion, the heron suddenly vanished underwater. Duma flinched and stared. His instincts told him there were dark hungry jaws lurking under that water—big ones!

At last Xan was ready to test his raft. He set his backpack on it and hung his CD player around his neck. Mashaka lifted his head out of the pack, eyeing the situation. Xan pushed the raft into the water and climbed on. It sank down six inches underwater.

"*Eek*," Mashaka complained.

Duma paced nervously on the bank.

"Chill. I'm not done yet," said Xan. He jumped into the water and pushed the raft back ashore. He made some adjustments.

Duma saw an eerie swirl of movement in the water downstream. He backed away.

Xan tried to coax him onto the raft. "Come on, Duma, everybody's waiting."

Duma sat down, stubbornly.

Xan patted the raft. "Get on. You can do it.

You're not going to get wet."

Duma refused to budge.

"Okay," said Xan, nonchalantly. "We're going. You stay here." He pushed off from shore and pretended to be paddling away.

Duma was unmoved.

Frustrated, Xan pushed the raft back. *"Duma! Get on now!"* he ordered.

Duma sank closer to the ground, looking more worried than ever.

Xan tried his sweetest voice instead. "Please, please, please," he coaxed. "We're almost there. I have to do this. Don't you want to go?"

Finally, Duma rose and took a step toward the raft. He put one foot in the water and pulled it out.

"You can do it, Duma," said Xan. "I'm not going to let anything happen to you."

Duma put one paw on the raft and then another. It seemed to hold him. He eased himself on all the way.

Xan pushed the raft into deeper water and began to swim, propelling and guiding it from behind. He aimed for a good landing point on the opposite shore, but the strong current pulled them downstream. Xan kicked harder. As he pushed against the raft, his CD player clicked on and loud rap music blared out across the swamp.

A few yards downstream a dozing crocodile opened his eyes and blinked in their direction. Xan felt the current getting stronger, sweeping them downstream faster and faster. Roaring rapids battered the flimsy raft until the cloth strips holding it together began to tear. No matter how hard he kicked, Xan couldn't steer the raft anymore—it was out of control! They smashed up against a big rock, and Xan and Duma went flailing into the water. The booming CD player was snagged by a branch, while the backpack sank to the bottom of the river like a stone. Xan clung desperately to the spear and swam up to the surface.

He spotted the big croc sliding into the river. He stabbed at it with his spear. *Whoosh! Chomp!* The music stopped abruptly. Xan looked just in time to see the croc gulping down the last dangling wires of his headphones. He grabbed Duma and swam hard, pulling him along with all his might. As soon as they could get their footing, the two of them shot out of the water and scrambled up the bank.

Drenched and gasping for breath, Xan put his arms around the bedraggled cheetah. "We made it.

We . . . Mashaka! Where's Mashaka?!"

Xan heard familiar chattering overhead. "Mashaka!" he shouted happily. The agile bush baby had leaped up into the overhanging branches of a tree.

Exhausted and humbled by the river, Xan sighed and picked up his spear. There was nothing to do now but press on. He looked up at the clouds moving across the sky. "Weather here moves east to west. We'll follow the clouds," he said decisively.

Mashaka rode on his shoulder, picking insects out of his hair.

"You can eat anything you find in there," quipped Xan.

12

As they left the river behind, they entered a whole new world of towering palm trees and thick stands of papyrus. Herds of swamp antelope and gazelles grazed in the grassy glens, and elephant families milled around the numerous waterways.

"Hey, is a zebra a white horse with black stripes or a black horse with white stripes?" Xan was chuckling to himself, delighted with this new, abundant landscape. He turned to give Duma a pat. But Duma had walked off to be on his own, sniffing the air, his eyes alert and searching.

Xan was proud of him. "A place with many teeth. Ha!" he cried. "It's a buffet! Duma, go get 'em!"

With just the slightest feeling of uneasiness, Xan watched Duma's long tail disappear into the grass. "Careful," he said to Mashaka, "we're on the menu, too."

As the two went on, the ground became squishy once again. Xan felt as if the mud might suck the shoes right off his feet. The vegetation was so thick, it became difficult to see very far ahead. Duma paused and waited for them to catch up.

Slogging their way out of the swampy area, they saw the vegetation grow thinner, and they found themselves face-to-face with an angry herd of cape buffalo. They lowered their hefty battering-ram horns and glared at Duma. Xan froze.

The buffalo began to charge. "Don't run, *don't run!*" Xan shouted. But it was no use. Duma and Mashaka ran. Mashaka grabbed a low-hanging branch and swung himself up into a tree. The herd thundered past below him, with Duma ahead of them, vanishing into the green.

"Duma! Duma!" Xan called. But in the wake of the buffalo, the swamp was as hushed as a church. Xan set off in the direction Duma had gone, calling and calling his name.

As the sun went down, Xan could hear the night hunters beginning to stir. Crocodiles floated down the moonlit river, circling wide around the enormous, bellowing hippos. Out on the savannah, a pack of hyenas gnawed the bones of a zebra they had recently hunted down. Lions stalked in to intimidate the hyenas and chase them away from their kill.

"Duma! Duma!" With each step Xan felt more lost and afraid. With each shout he called more attention to himself—an easy target. A shadowy figure trotted toward him through the grass. Quickly Xan took the cue from Mashaka and scrambled up the nearest tree. Wedging his body in the fork of a branch, he pointed the trembling tip of Rip's spear down at the dark shape. It paused below him—it looked like a lion.

Xan felt the eight tickling legs of a tree spider crawling up his arm. He held his breath and tried not to move. The spider crept across his face. Xan's cheek twitched. He wanted desperately to scream and swat it away, but then the lion would surely spot him. Slowly, slowly, he reached up to his face, plucked off the creepy crawler, and set it on its way. Xan braced himself for the lion's pounce. But something in the grass caught its attention instead. The dark shape moved away, and Xan began to breathe again. He was relieved, but badly shaken.

The moment his feet touched the ground, something flew at him like a bat with bony fingers. *"Aahhhhhhh!"* Xan screamed in spite of himself. But it was just Mashaka, crawling up his shirt and blinking at him with his wide, frightened eyes.

Some distance away, Duma's ears perked up. Had he heard a familiar voice? He couldn't be sure. The nighttime cacophony of the swamp seemed to swallow it up. He moved silently, trying to make himself invisible under the moonlit bushes. An interesting scent caught his attention, and he followed it into a bower of trees. He saw something familiar—it looked like a fence. No, it was a rectangular box made of metal like a fence. And inside was a fragrant piece of raw meat! With no fear, Duma rushed in. *Clang!* The trap sprang shut. Duma pushed frantically against the door, but it wouldn't budge; he tried to press his head through the steel wires, but they were too tight. Terrified, he began to chirp, just as he had done for his mama so long ago.

But Xan didn't hear him. His own shouting had startled a warthog, and the massive beast was coming straight at him. Xan screamed and ran heedlessly through the bushes—the monster right behind him—tusks gleaming. He jumped over a log and scrambled across slippery rocks. His foot slid on a patch of moss and he fell, headfirst down into a deep ditch, and *thud*! Everything went black.

13

Xan awoke to the sound of Duma purring. Slowly, groggily, he opened his eyes, and in the glare of the firelight he saw Duma looking back at him. Big, dark fingers reached down to scratch the cheetah's head. He heard a familiar voice.

"Xan, are you there?"

A very muddy and exhausted-looking Rip was smiling down gently at him.

"What happened?" Xan murmured.

"You're both alive!" cried Rip. "I am very happy for that!"

"You found Duma!" Xan cried.

"In a poacher's trap," said Rip, "and you in a hog's house. But that is a lot better than a lion's belly."

Xan rubbed his aching head. "How did you get across the river? And find us?"

"You left big tracks. I came down across the bridge." He pointed over his shoulder. "Right down there."

Xan groaned and closed his eyes again.

Rip smiled. He patted Duma and went off to pick some fruit. When he returned, he and Xan decided to eat their breakfast on the trail. Rip carved a slice of fruit and handed to Xan. He made a face at the bitter taste and chewy texture, but he was starving! He put out his hand for more.

"I'm sorry for what I did. It was a big mistake," said Xan.

"But you were right. I was thinking of how much money I could get for you both," said Rip. "I had big plans. I left my village, my wife, and my children to try to be a big man. I went to the big city to make big money. But soon, I was a small man. I had to steal to eat, and I ended up in the biggest jail you ever saw. I won't go back there ever again."

Rip leaned over and handed something to Xan. It was his mother's talisman!

"It fell from your pocket," Rip explained. "Do you know what it is?"

"My mother gave it to me," said Xan.

"It is an object of power." Rip pointed to the

eyeholes on the small mask. "It means you should look at something through different eyes—maybe you see different things—maybe you feel different things. How you look can lead to sadness—or to happiness."

They walked along in silence for a while, Xan fingering the talisman with new appreciation and thinking about his mom.

"My mom probably hates me. I left her . . . ran away to do this."

"Mothers never stop loving their children," said Rip.

Xan glanced at him skeptically. "You're not a mother."

"No, I am a father." Rip looked away, worried that Xan might judge him for deserting his family.

"Where you want to go, they are making a big

new road. There is a better place for Duma. A day's walk from my village. It's very wild . . . beautiful! I'll show you."

Xan smiled at Rip. "Why not?"

Rip clapped his hands together, delighted. "*Yebo* . . . Why not!"

As the four pals continued across the wide Okavango Delta, Duma spotted a herd of impala at a watering hole up ahead. He crouched down to stalk them. Closer and closer he crept, moving silently through the grass. One of the impala lifted his head and saw Duma. The impala sprinted away, with the whole herd following it at top speed. Duma went into overdrive, and in seconds he had overtaken one.

Xan and Rip jumped up and down and cheered.

The impala zigzagged left and right trying to outmaneuver the cat. Duma sprang and the impala went down.

Xan and Rip whooped, "Hooray!" They waited for Duma to deliver the killing bite.

Instead . . . he started licking the impala.

"What?!" cried Xan in disbelief.

Rip closed his eyes and shook his head.

Xan ran to Duma, took his head in his hands, and stared right into his eyes. *"Bite! Bite!"* he ordered. "You're a hunter! A *hunter!*"

▲ ▽ ▲ ▽ ▲ ▽ ▲ ▽ ▲ ▽ ▲ ▽ ▲ ▽

14

Rip was still chuckling that evening when they parted the bushes to find a truly bizarre sight. Glimmering under romantic torchlight was an exclusive five-star safari lodge. Tourists in clean khaki clothes were dancing to the tunes of Frank Sinatra and feasting on all kinds of gourmet food!

Rip grinned through the bushes. "That food is an easy catch."

"And I know how," replied Xan.

The next morning, the tourists gathered at the riverside to do some bird-watching. They boarded a floating observation platform, which was moored to the riverbank near the boat docks. Rip and Xan sauntered over.

Rip held a long, dark snake out toward Xan. "Ready?" he whispered.

Xan nodded. *"Help! Help me!"* he shouted.

The tourists began to peer out from the floating bird blind, wondering what was going on. "There's a boy hurt out there!" cried one.

"It bit me! Help!" cried Xan.

A white-haired man rushed out of the blind, shouting, "I'm a doctor! Bring him here!"

Rip, who had slipped quietly into the water, held onto the edge of the platform and watched as Xan was carried in.

Xan moaned and thrashed dramatically. "It bit me, bit me," he murmured.

"What bit you?" asked the doctor, kneeling down beside him

"This . . ." Xan tore open his shirt, and the snake slithered out.

"It's a black mamba!" shouted Rip from his hiding place.

The tourists panicked. Everyone stampeded to the lodge and cowered inside in terror. Xan tossed the harmless snake into the water, and he and Rip folded the tourists' entire brunch up into the crisp white tablecloth the food was laying upon and carried it off. They untied a canoe from the dock, tossed their treasure in, and paddled away up the river.

Rip laughed heartily as Xan pulled treats out of

their "bag." "You will go far, Xan . . . as long as you can stay out of jail!"

"Here!" Xan tossed Rip a bagel with lox and horseradish sauce.

Rip examined it suspiciously. "What's that stuff there?"

"It's good!" cried Xan. "A special kind of fish."

"Yeah . . . it's good for you, huh? You think?" Rip studied the bagel. "Well . . . if it's good for the big rich boys . . ." He took a bite and grinned. "It's even better for me!"

Duma got to work on a big leg of lamb.

Mashaka was delighted with the shrimp salad.

"How about this?" Xan laughed, handing Rip a cold pork chop with a frilly paper skirt on the bone.

"Oh yeah? What's this mean?" Rip tickled the

little skirt. "It dances in your belly?" He made the chop dance along on his paddle. "Tickles your ribs!" he cried.

"Hey," said Xan. "I got something else for you." He fished Hock's big wad of money out of his pocket and held it out for Rip.

"What's this?" said Rip, suddenly getting serious.

"I want you to have it," said Xan.

"Oh . . . no . . . I can't."

"Don't be a bonehead," said Xan. "Take it. What is it? Just a bunch of paper."

"No, man. People die for this stuff. I can't. . . ."

"I want you to have it . . . for helping me."

Rip shook his head.

Xan held the money up in the air, as if to let it fly away in the wind. "Okay, you've got five seconds! Five, four, three, two . . ."

Rip grabbed the money. "Okay. I'll get you out of trouble one more time."

He grinned, taking a plastic water bottle out of his pocket. He poured what looked to Xan like a bunch of dirt and gravel into the palm of his hand.

"I found these pretty little rocks the other day . . . when I dug myself out," he said.

Xan stared at the small, triangular, almost translucent rocks in the dirt. He wondered if they were diamonds.

Rip offered him one. "You take that one to remember old Rip, who is now going to leave you." He reached his arms around his head, twisting his neck, and making a sickening crunch. He slumped over, face forward.

"Rip! What's wrong?"

Rip gasped. "It's the money!"

"Rip, speak to me!"

Rip opened his eyes and made the horrible crunching sound again. Xan realized it was just Rip squeezing the plastic bottle full of money. And the two of them fell over laughing, while Duma and Mashaka looked on.

15

Full and content, they poled slowly up the Okavango Delta in their canoe, enjoying the sun and the quiet water. Farther and farther north they went, until the river finally became too fast and shallow. There, they beached the canoe and, carrying what was left of their provisions, began to hike across the savannah, toward the peaks of the Erongo Mountains.

Xan kept an eye out for Duma, who now loved to roam ahead. One afternoon, Xan spotted him on a rocky outcrop exploring the carcass of a freshly killed gemsbok. Once Duma had tasted the blood, he started to tear hungrily at the meat.

Rip and Xan approached.

"Lions kill it . . . not long ago," said Rip, taking out his spear.

Xan reached down to cut off a hindquarter. "Come on, Duma. We can share this."

Duma growled menacingly and pulled the carcass away.

Xan stood back, surprised. "Duma, you're being a pig!"

"Leave him and be happy, Xan. It's the meat he knows in his bones from way back. After he's had his fill, then it will be our turn." Rip looked around. "Just hope the lions don't come back. . . ."

By dusk Xan and Rip had packed up their

hindquarter and hiked across a vast escarpment to a red rock cave Rip knew well. "My father brought me here when I was younger than you," he said. "It is here that I saw there was more to him and to me than I ever knew."

From the mouth of the cave they looked out across dry, rocky watercourses and beautiful golden plains. Inside the cave, Rip showed Xan ancient paintings of dream hunts and native gods.

Rip built a campfire, and they roasted their share of the lions' kill. The firelight flickered on the cave walls, illuminating the paintings with a glowing presence.

"These old ones talk to me," said Rip. "I feel how they lived, what they feared, who they loved. The world they knew is gone, but we are not so different."

Xan was transfixed. He had never seen anything like this artwork.

"No one comes here anymore. They are forgotten," Rip continued. "I am no better. My own father, I don't know if he lives or not."

"My dad . . . he died," said Xan, choking back tears. "How can someone just—disappear—forever?"

"I would be angry, too," said Rip.

They sat together in silence.

Finally, Rip sighed. "People go when *they* are ready, not you."

Duma moved over and snuggled down at Xan's feet.

"We are all travelers on the same river," said Rip. "Grandparents, then parents, then their own sons and daughters. Each of us is a part of everything and everyone who came before. We all have our time on the river. We do what we can before we disappear."

Xan looked up at Rip and nodded. He thought he understood what Rip was trying to say—some of it at least.

"Xan, this is your time," Rip declared. "Duma's, too. And mine."

He turned the meat over on the fire and did some thinking. "We'll soon be where Duma is going," he said. "After—then I see my family. See if they welcome me. Then, you can go be with your mother. That will be good. Your father is dead for her, too."

Xan wasn't so sure his mother would welcome him. "It's different now," he said. "Everything's changed."

"Change. That's it. That's what happens—all the time." Rip paused for a second. "But we change, too."

Xan reached out to stroke Duma's head. Change. *Yes,* he thought sadly, *things are always changing.*

16

Seasoned travelers, Xan and Rip strode confidently across the golden plains of Koakoland. Duma roamed freely, checking in with his human companions now and then.

Excited, Xan stopped and pointed far ahead. "Below that cliff, in the canyon. See? A village!"

Rip nodded, smiling. He was about to say something about it, when he caught sight of a big, vaporous red cloud swarming up ahead. His smile dropped.

Worried, Xan followed his gaze. "What?" he demanded.

"*Tsetse!*" Rip took off at a dead run. "*Run, man. Go! Go!*"

But the red cloud was faster. Soon it was floating over their heads. It dropped down on them like a horrible fishing net. Billions of tiny red bugs covered their bodies like quivering fur. Buzzing and biting, the insects wriggled into their hair and eyes and ears and noses. They slapped and ran and swatted at the bugs, but it was no use. The cloud of tsetse flies lifted off only when they'd had their fill.

Even after they'd gone, Mashaka kept shricking, and Duma hopped around from the pain of the bites.

"Duma, stop," soothed Xan. "You're okay."

But Rip was in a panic. "We must hurry now," he ordered.

As storm clouds wrapped the Erongo Mountains in their mist, Rip stumbled desperately ahead.

"Rip?" asked Xan, confused.

Exhausted and wheezing, Rip plopped down on a rock.

Xan was shocked to see Rip's hands trembling and his face horribly swollen. Instinctively, Xan reached up to touch his own face.

"You're okay," panted Rip, "but a long time ago, I got sick from tsetse. Bad. Real bad."

Duma looked frightened and distraught. Rip noticed and followed the cheetah's gaze to the top of a high ridge. In their flailing and desperation, they'd attracted the attention of a pride of lions.

"They see us," whispered Xan.

"Fire. We've got to build a fire," gasped Rip.

They scrambled to collect wood. But clouds had gathered overhead and a drenching rain was soon soaking the twigs and branches.

As darkness fell, Xan saw the lions moving down from their ridge into the tall, concealing grass. Rip crouched down trying to shield their kindling twigs from the rain.

Xan tried to ignite them with his lighter, but the wood was already too wet. "We need something dry," he muttered.

Rip cut open one of his water bottles and pulled out the wad of money.

"No!" cried Xan.

Rip ignored him. He put a few dry bills under the kindling. "Light it!" he ordered.

Xan hesitated for a moment, then touched the lighter's flame to the money. A curl of smoke went up. Rip blew on it gently. He added more bills and the flames jumped up, drying out the kindling and igniting the larger branches. Xan hurried to add more wood. Slowly and steadily the fire grew, and the rain dwindled to a stop. They sat back and sighed in relief.

But Rip was looking awful. His eyes had swollen nearly shut. He lay back, wheezing, hardly able to take a breath. Deep down, Xan knew his friend would not last the night without medicine to calm his allergic reaction. He piled more sticks on the fire and laid Rip's spear by his side.

Rip sensed what he was up to. "Don't go. Please. It's too dangerous," he pleaded.

"I'm not going to let you die," declared Xan. He

turned to Duma with a grave expression. "You have to stay. Protect these guys."

Duma looked up at him, worried, but uncomprehending.

With only a fire torch for light and protection, Xan started off at a brisk pace. Duma tried to follow. "Stay, Duma," Xan ordered. "They need you. I'm serious. *Stay*."

Duma sat. Rip shivered, feverish, too sick to protest anymore.

As Xan moved silently through the bush, the moon appeared out of the clouds, and cast the Erongo Mountains in an eerie light. It also illuminated Xan. Two dark shapes trotted behind him in the grass.

Duma paced around the fire, staring out into the darkness. He was afraid to leave the safety of the fire; nevertheless, his instincts would not allow him to leave his best friend alone and unprotected. He tore off after Xan at top speed, leaving Mashaka curled up next to Rip.

As he emerged from a dark wood, Xan could see firelights flickering in the village up ahead. He rushed on—rustling and crunching through the fallen leaves—unaware that the lions had him in their sights. And they were closing in fast!

Suddenly, Duma streaked across their path. Attracted by the fast-moving prey, the lions veered off after the cheetah. Duma raced back through the woods, the lions close behind him. Deliberately luring them away from his friend, Duma zigzagged through a rocky area and ducked into a small cave. One of the lions scrunched in behind him. The passageway narrowed. Duma could see a dim light ahead—a small opening! It was just big enough for Duma to squeeze through, but too small for the lion. The lion roared in frustration as Duma escaped back into the forest.

When he was far enough away, Duma lay down to rest. But a familiar chirping sound—a sound from his distant past—brought him to his feet again. He sniffed the air. He looked around and there in the bushes, staring right back at him, was another cheetah. They stood perfectly still. Duma let out a long, low growl. The other cheetah stood his ground. Duma flattened his ears and approached cautiously. The cheetah loped away, but not far. Duma sniffed the ground where the other had been. When he lifted his eyes, he saw the cheetah was studying him again. Duma moved forward, and this time the cheetah let him approach.

This new cheetah was bigger than Duma, and Duma was uncertain exactly what to do. He circled around a few times. The new cheetah made the first move—he nuzzled Duma and licked his mouth—the customary greeting for friends. Duma caught on quickly. He nuzzled the new cheetah back and licked his mouth. Before long they were chasing, nipping, tumbling, and playing like old friends.

17

A while later, still completely oblivious of his close escape from the lions, Xan entered the village. He saw an old man coming out of one of the larger huts. His halo of white hair seemed to glow in the moonlight.

"We need help! Doctor!" cried Xan.

The old man watched quizzically as Xan tried to mime their trouble with the biting insects and Rip's subsequent fever. "Out there is a man—very sick—bitten—he's puffed up," said Xan, puffing up his cheeks and gesturing with his hands.

The old man nodded knowingly. "Tsetse."

He called for three strong men to help Xan carry the sick man up to the village. When they arrived, Rip's face was so swollen, Xan could barely recognize him. After a long, painful trek back, the men laid Rip down in the medicine woman's hut.

Xan set Rip's spear by the door, patted Mashaka, and watched the medicine woman boil up a strong yellow liquid. The old man assisted her, adding special leaves to the potion. Satisfied that Rip was in good hands, he began to worry about Duma.

He ventured out of the village as far as he dared. "Duma! *Duma?!*" he called into the darkness. But the cheetah did not answer his call.

Xan spent a restless night. In the morning he watched the village come to life. The people stared at Xan, saying nothing. Xan felt a deep sense of wonder at the fact that this strange remote village was a real part of his world. A young boy came over and smiled warmly.

"I'm Xan," said Xan.

The boy touched Xan's golden hair, then reached out to pet Mashaka.

"*Eek!*" Mashaka screeched. But he wasn't afraid of the boy—he saw something in the distance.

Xan followed his gaze. A cheetah! It was Duma—it must be! He raced to the crest of a hill and scanned the landscape. In the vast grassland below he could see giraffes, elephants, zebra, antelope—everything but cheetahs! Discouraged, he was about to head back to the village when he caught sight of something that held him absolutely spellbound: Duma and another cheetah racing each other across the plain!

Xan lay down on the hilltop to watch. Duma and his new friend lay down to rest together in the shade of a tree. Soon a small herd of antelope caught their interest and they stood up, alert. Xan stood up, too, not wanting to miss a thing. The antelope sensed the hunters nearby and bolted. Instinctively, Duma knew to split away from his friend. The two of them zeroed in on one straggler and came at the antelope from both sides.

Xan jumped up and down, shouting, "Go! Go! Go!"

Like an arrow shot from a bow, Duma struck first, knocking the animal to the ground. With a quick flash of teeth, the cheetah dealt the death bite, and it was all over—Duma had made his first kill. He looked up in Xan's direction, as if waiting for praise.

Seeing Duma like that, something in Xan finally let go. For the first time he was able to see what his dad had seen in Duma all along—that Duma belonged to this wilderness more than he had ever belonged to them. Xan had done what he needed to do—he had brought his best friend home.

As the sun went down, Xan decided it was time to go. Duma and his new friend still lay by their kill. Xan longed for a different kind of good-bye, but he knew he must leave the cheetah to his new life.

"Bye, Duma," he said softly. He rose and headed down the hill to the village, bravely holding back his tears.

▼ ▲ ▼

Back in the village that night, Xan turned a corner around one of the huts, and there was Duma, standing before him. Xan hugged his friend and buried his face in his fur. But then he remembered what he had come there for. He held Duma's head in his hands one last time and gazed into his eyes.

"Take care of yourself," he whispered.

He turned and walked away, struggling not to look back, so as not to confuse Duma about which way he should go. Duma followed Xan with his eyes, uncertain—the evening wind ruffling his fur. Slowly he turned and loped back up the hill where his new friend was waiting for him.

Back in the medicine hut, the old woman was busy removing the now-hardened mud pack she had plastered all over Rip's face. The poultice had

heavily on a wooden staff. A woman came in beside him, just as old but even more frail. Xan saw Rip's eyes filling with tears. He didn't have to hear Rip say it to know that they were his parents. Still weak from his illness, Rip stood up to embrace them.

Xan looked on, overcome with thoughts of his own parents. He turned away, tears finally falling freely down his face. He'd said good-bye to his father, and to Duma. Now, he knew, it was time to go home.

With Mashaka sitting high on his shoulder, Xan said his good-byes and headed east, into the rising sun. Rip accompanied him to the edge of the village. The friends embraced, and Xan was on his way. He paused at the top of the hill to scan for Duma. There he was, resting in the shade of a big rock outcrop! Hearing Xan's familiar footfall, Duma looked up and regarded his old friend one last time. The boy and the cheetah had grown up together. Now it was time for them to begin their adult lives.

▲ ▼ ▲ ▼ ▲ ▼ ▲ ▼ ▲ ▼ ▲ ▼ ▲ ▼

18

Ever since Xan left, Kristin had been trying to tend the Van der Bok farm by herself. She was in her work pants, all spattered with mud from the day's plowing, driving the old tractor back to the barn for the evening, when she saw a familiar figure standing at the bottom of the long driveway.

"*Xan?!*" she cried. She jumped off the tractor and ran to him. "*Xan!*"

"*Mom!*" he shouted, running up the driveway toward her.

Kristin slowed to a stop and stared. He was alive! And how he had changed! Taller, stronger—wiser-looking as well. She could see all the changes in his face.

Xan hesitated, wondering if she was angry with him. He noticed her work clothes and callused hands. She had changed, too. She was a farmer now—everything about her showed it.

Xan fought back the tears. "I had to go," he sobbed, "Duma . . ."

"Where is he?"

"In the mountains."

His mother reached out to wrap him in her arms. Tears welled up in her eyes as she imagined how hard it must have been for him—dealing with his father's death and saying good-bye to Duma, too. "I'm sorry I didn't understand," she said.

Mashaka tugged on Xan's pant leg and chattered happily. Still holding his mom close, he smiled his father's mischievous smile. "Mom, without looking. What shoes are you wearing?"

Kristin smiled through her tears. "Boots?"

They looked down, laughing at Mashaka and at the muddy boots on her feet. Xan pulled the talisman from his pocket and placed it in his mother's hand. And they walked, arm in arm, up the long driveway toward home.

There are things you know without knowing. Things you carry in your blood and bones like a memory. For Duma, it was his wildness. For Rip, his village. For Xan, everything his dad believed in and loved was alive in him.

While Xan was taking Duma to the mountains,

Duma was taking Xan somewhere, too. Finding Duma's true home brought Xan back to his. And it showed him that love doesn't stop when time passes, or you live in different places, or when somebody is gone.